Long Sleeves

Story by
Lady Canaday

Illustrations by
Joshua Allen

AuthorHouse™
1663 Liberty Drive
Bloomington, IN 47403
www.authorhouse.com
Phone: 1-800-839-8640

Published by AuthorHouse: 08/26/2015

ISBN: 978-1-5049-0789-7 (hc)
ISBN: 978-1-4969-3448-2 (sc)
ISBN: 978-1-4969-3449-9 (e)

Library of Congress Control Number: 2014914533

Print information available on the last page.

This book is printed on acid-free paper.

authorHOUSE®

Mr. Marcoscaife is a beloved third grade teacher at William H. Thomas Elementary School in Baton Rouge, Louisiana. He teaches eight and nine-year-old kids. On the first day of the 2012-2013 school year, Mr. Marcoscaife tells his bright-eyed and bushy-tailed students why he uses a wheelchair. Mr. Marcoscaife says, "My grandmother, Grandma Mamie, always told her grandchildren not to play around the stairs at her home because we could hurt ourselves and get in big trouble. When I was about your age, my baby brother Larell and I were wrestling in our grandma's upstairs hallway. First, we annihilated our great-grandma Dibby's vintage crystal bud vase when it fell off the hall table. Shortly thereafter, we completely demolished our great-great-grandma Sang's antique stained glass lamp when it hit the hardwood floor. Both items shattered into a million particles, but that didn't stop us. We kept wrestling until I fell down the spiral staircase and injured my lower back. Since then, walking has been challenging for me. I use an electric wheelchair to get around quickly. I'm living proof that you should always listen to your grandparents because serious injuries can occur when you're disobdient."

Carlos raises his hand and asks, "If you weren't banged up, would you guys have gotten a lecture and grounded *like white kids* or gotten a butt whipping *like black kids*?" Caucasian teacher laughs for a moment and says, "Probably all of the above. Speaking of discipline, I'll tell the class a funny story. About a week before my accident, my brother and I got in trouble for stealing potato chips from a mom-and-pop store. When the two of us got caught **red-handed**, we knew a spanking was the foremost thing on old-school Grandma Mamie's to-do list. We were shocked when she grabbed her thickest belt for a butt whipping. Just as Grandma Mamie got ready to give us the first whop, her stomach started bubbling loudly from the whole batch of homemade peanut butter cookie dough she had eaten before we arrived. Also, the arthritis in Grandma Mamie's hands was so bad that every time she swung the belt, she shook uncontrollably and ended up whipping herself." Children giggle. Mr. Marcoscaife says, "After the attempted butt-whipping fiasco, Grandma Mamie gave us an in-your-face lecture and grounded us until our parents came to pick us up."

First day back from winter break, Mr. Marcoscaife displays in his classroom a charity calendar that shows him fishing. Wednesday, August 14, 2013, is circled with a **red** marker. Also in that space, it says: my birthday and has a happy face underneath. The fundraising campaign featured men and women with different hobbies who're physically challenged. It raised a ton of money for the Special Olympics.

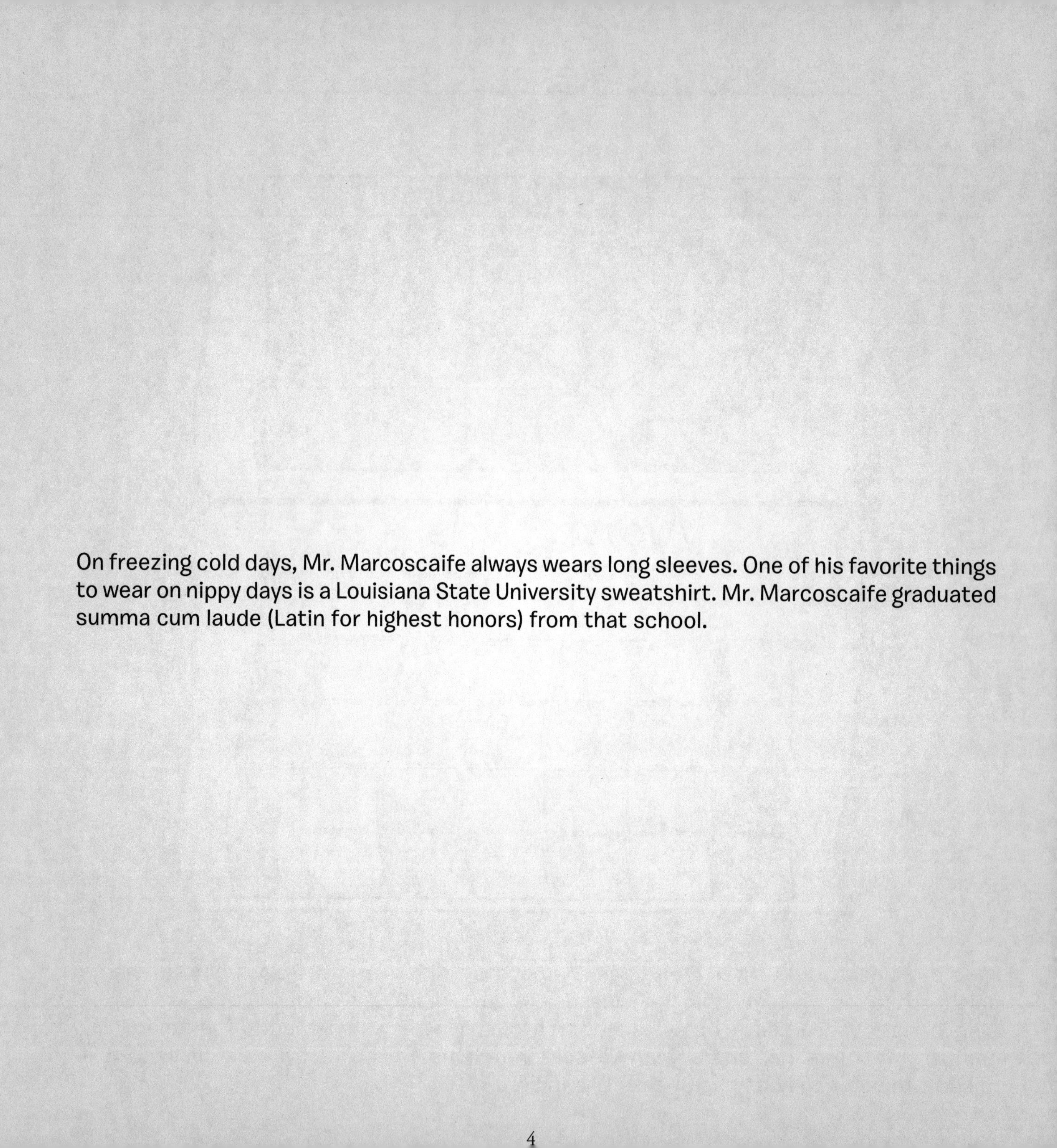

On freezing cold days, Mr. Marcoscaife always wears long sleeves. One of his favorite things to wear on nippy days is a Louisiana State University sweatshirt. Mr. Marcoscaife graduated summa cum laude (Latin for highest honors) from that school.

On windy days, whether it's breezy or a gusty wind storm, Mr. Marcoscaife always wears long sleeves. Today, he's wearing a **black** Windbreaker with long sleeves. When Mr. Marcoscaife goes outside, he wears wraparound shades to protect the lamp of the body (his eyes) and covers his head with the hood to protect his hair from dust.

On rainy days, whether it's drizzling or a downpour with rumbling thunder, Mr. Marcoscaife always wears long sleeves and his umbrella hat when he's outside. If the local meteorologists (weather scientists) forecast rain for the next school day, class gets a tasty treat. It may be piña colada yogurt, piña colada cake or a virgin piña colada drink. Whether the class eats yummy yogurt, chows down creamy cake or sips on their bliss beverage with umbrella straws, everyone chillaxes and listens to the instrumental version of "Escape (The Piña Colada Song)" by Rupert Holmes.

On scorching hot days with triple-digit heat, Mr. Marcoscaife always wears long sleeves. Today, he's wearing a long sleeve shirt with vertical **red**-and-**white** lines.

Mr. Marcoscaife has a student named Kevin. Everybody calls him **"Chili Red"** because of his curly **auburn** hair. One midafternoon, **Chili Red** says to his teenage brother, Ronald, "Mr. Marcoscaife was your third grade teacher. Why does he always wear long sleeves?" Ronald strokes his chin and answers, "That's a good question. I doubt Mr. Marcoscaife is concealing a full sleeve nudie tat of his biker babe like Uncle Richard. Perhaps he's just waiting for 2014 when Obamacare kicks in so he can fix his arms."

Week before school ends, **Chili Red** asks Mr. Marcoscaife in front of the entire class, "Why do you always wear long sleeves no matter what the weather is?" Teacher replies, "When you go home today, I want everybody to think about a guess for tomorrow."

Next day, kids are antsy and want to play the guessing game right away. First, Mr. Marcoscaife calls roll. After that, he says, "As you can tell by my special **green** shirt with **black** question marks, I'm excited to see if someone comes up with the correct answer. Keep in mind that the reason I always wear long sleeves has *nothing* to do with why I use a wheelchair."

Woody Woo starts the guessing game. He raises his hand and guesses, "Your arms were burned in a fire while trying to save a **blue-haired** old lady and her kitty cat from their burning home." Mr. Marcoscaife replies, "No. I'm not *that* courageous. If I saw something like that I'd call 9-1-1 and pray the senior citizen and her feline are safely rescued."

Wisdom raises her hand and guesses, "You have really thin skin plus your green veins are long and slimy like the okra in my nana's nasty gumbo." Mr. Marcoscaife smiles and says, "No. That's not it. Speaking of the okra fruit, can anyone name the shell of the okra? I'll give you a hint. The shell of a pea has the same name." Class replies, "Pod." Mr. Marcoscaife states, "Whole okra can be 2-7 inches long and shaped like a finger. If you ever heard anyone refer to okra as lady fingers, now you know why."

Julayne raises her hand and guesses, "You have a rash that's not contagious, but it's frightening to little kids." Mr. Marcoscaife replies, "Nope."

Dion raises his hand and guesses, "You have weird-looking goose bumps that never went away." Mr. Marcoscaife says, "No."

Morgan raises her hand and guesses, "Maybe it's because you're really hairy like a gorilla and my daddy." Mr. Marcoscaife chuckles and replies, "Nope."

Justin raises his hand and guesses, "You were in the arny in Afghan, got shot and your arms are riddled with bullet holes as big as miniature marshmallows, Life Savers or jumbo cotton balls." Mr. Marcoscaife says, "No. Before anyone else gets any more *hole* ideas, I want everybody to know that my arms don't look like two slices of Swiss cheese or SpongeBob SquarePants. I wasn't a brave soldier who courageously risked my life in the *army* in *Afghanistan*. By the way, an Afghan is a tall dog from Afghanistan known for its long silky coat and small brain." Next, the teacher shows the class a picture of an Afghan from the World Wide Web. After that, Mr. Marcoscaife states, "I'd like to go back to the candy subject for a minute. Does anybody know why Life Savers have a hole in the center?" Children shrug their shoulders and stick out their bottom lips. Mr. Marcoscaife explains, "The hole was put there as a safety precaution so kids wouldn't choke on the candy."

Tyana raises her hand and guesses, “You have extra wormy mop hair growing on your arms. It’s so thick and long, we can play double Dutch with it.” Mr. Marcoscaife smiles and says, “I don’t have dreadlocks growing on my arms. My ‘wormy mop hair’ is called dreadlocks or dreads for short.”

Kenji raises his hand and guesses, "You burned yourself while frying chicken. That happened to my mom one time when hot oil popped onto her arm. After she got burned, she said a really bad word in Japanese." Mr. Marcoscaife replies, "No. That's not the reason either."

Ta'Mya raises her hand and guesses, "You got a bad sunburn at the beach because you ran out of sunscreen or you stayed on a tanning bed way too long like Tan Mom. Now you're stuck with burnt **orange** skin." Mr. Marcoscaife says, "None of those scenarios happened."

King raises his hand and guesses, "You got freckles so big that they look like pepperoni slices." Mr. Marcoscaife smiles and replies, "No. I'm glad I don't because it would be hard for me not to eat them." Kids laugh. Mr. Marcoscaife asks, "What kind of meat is pepperoni?" Class answers, "Sausage." Mr. Marcoscaife says, "Very good. The Italian sausage is a combination of beef and pork. It's also hard, dry, spicy, and looks like an edible checker."

My'lah raises her hand and guesses, "You keep a secret treasure map hidden up your sleeve so that the drunk pirates at Disneyland won't steal it." Mr. Marcoscaife replies, "I wish I did. My lovely wife and I would be filthy rich like Richie Rich. We could retire and take a trip around the world."

Duane raises his hand and guesses, “You got ripped by eating tons of canned spinach like Popeye the Sailor Man. So, you wear long sleeves to keep the lady teachers from swooning over you like you’re a rock star. It also prevents them from gawking and drooling at your big bulging biceps until their beady eyes pop out of their heads.” Mr. Marcoscaife states, “Some of the staff call me nicknames like ‘Buff Stuff,’ ‘Chester,’ ‘Beef Cake,’ and my fave, ‘Hot Bod.’ If you were right about the lady teachers drooling, I’d keep a stack of adult bibs in my back wheelchair pocket.”

Anthony raises his hand and guesses, “You got creepy moles as big as whole **black** olives.” Mr. Marcoscaife says, “I have a few moles here and there. Thankfully, they aren’t *that* large. Olives are a fruit which may be **black** or **green**. There’s also a furry **black** animal called a mole that’s known for its strong digging claws.”

Venetia raises her hand and guesses, “You have all the answers to *Jeopardy!* written with crayons and markers.” Mr. Marcoscaife replies, “Cheating is bad and wrong. My arms would have to be the size of all the bodies of water in the world to have *that* many answers.”

Yvonne raises her hand and guesses, “You have **brown**-and-**white** cow patches on both arms.” Mr. Marcoscaife says, “I don’t have the Vitiligo skin disease like Michael Jackson had. Just so everyone knows, calling the two-tone skin ‘cow patches’ is mean and hurts a person’s feelings who has Vitiligo.”

Johnny raises his hand and guesses, “You got that skin condition that starts with the letter E or that other one that starts with the letter P.” Mr. Marcoscaife replies, “I don’t have eczema or psoriasis.”

Kenny raises his hand and guesses, “Your elbows are so ashy, they look like powdered doughnuts.” Mr. Marcoscaife says, “No. Now I want a Krispy Kreme glazed doughnut that’s fresh from the oven.”

Denise raises her hand and guesses, “You got a birthmark or super-ugly tattoo that won’t wash off in a bath with Mr. Bubble.” Mr. Marcoscaife states, “No birthmark. I’m afraid of the tattoo machine. My dreads would stand straight up on my head like quills on a porcupine. I’d scream, cry like a baby and hope I don’t wee-wee on myself.”

John raises his hand and asks, “Why do people like to brand themselves with tattoos like they’re livestock on a ranch?” Mr. Marcoscaife answers, “People have different reasons for tattooing their skin. Speaking of skin, it’s the largest organ of the body. Personally, I think my skin is perfect just the way God made it.”

Sabrena raises her hand and guesses, “You have a bad scar on your arm that looks like a giant zipper, people tease you and ask a bunch of nosy questions.” Mr. Marcoscaife replies, “No. If that was true, I’d ask my talented wife, who is a makeup artist for a movie studio, to put makeup on it.”

Courtney raises his hand and says, “You always have nice things to say about your wife. She must not be a nagging ball and chain like my papa’s buddies always call my mama behind her back. You never told us whether or not your wife is a push girl and if you guys have kids.” Mr. Marcoscaife states, “My wife is a land walker and she’s the *total opposite* of ‘a nagging ball and chain.’ Sounds like your dad needs some new friends who don’t insult his spouse. My wife and I don’t have children.”

Ricky raises his hand and says, “Maybe she’s not ready to be a *real* parent. Have y’all tried being a pet parent?” Mr. Marcoscaife replies, “Yes. We’re the proud pooch parents of Blue and Louie, but that’s not the reason.”

Becky raises her hand and asks, “Are you not a *human* parent because you’re in a wheelchair?” Mr. Marcoscaife answers, “Men and women who use a wheelchair may make one, two, three or however many babies God blesses them to have. Wheelchair users may also be birth parents of twins and higher-order multiples ... triplets, quadruplets and so forth. The reason my sweetheart and I don’t have *real* kids is because she’s afraid of getting *really* fat.”

Leslie raises her hand and says, “Your wife could adopt like my barren cousin, Dana. That way, she can have a bunch of babies, give you a Happy Father’s Day card every year and still be a hot mom.”

Mimi raises her hand and guesses, “A mad scientist drugged you and stuffed your arms with elbow macaroni noodles.” Mr. Marcoscaife replies, “Nope. No sci-fi stuff.”

Brandy raises her hand and guesses, “You have pie secrets like that Snowden man on the news.” Mr. Marcoscaife states, “I’m no *spy* guy. Committing a **white-collar** crime, hiding in a foreign country and living in fear didn’t make my bucket list.”

Dynem raises her hand and guesses, “You got a gang of tiger stripes like my mommy has on her apron. That’s what she calls her jiggly jelly belly.” Mr. Marcoscaife says, “I don’t have *stretch marks*.”

Robby raises his hand and guesses, “You got those icky **purple** spider veins like wrinkly old people.” Mr. Marcoscaife replies, “No.”

Daniela raises her hand and guesses, “You like to cut yourself in private and cover up the marks from people like my loco cuzo in Mexico.” Mr. Marcoscaife says, “I would never do self-harm to my body. Sounds like your cousin is really sad about something happening in his or her life. I hope your relative gets help from a doctor as soon as possible.”

Mr. Marcoscaife sips on his water bottle. Seconds later, Davina raises her hand and states, “Ooh! Ooh! I got it. Your elbows are so dark that when they’re folded back, they look like my preggo mom’s boobies.” Teacher spits out the water, excuses himself and replies, “That’s *definitely* not the reason! My elbows don’t look like the darker area around our nipples called the areola.”

Mr. Marcoscaife asks, “Any more guesses?” Class answers, “No.” Mr. Marcoscaife says, “As everybody knows, I wear long sleeves throughout all four seasons: summer, fall/autumn, winter, and spring. Before I tell why I wear them year-round, I want to say that everyone came up with great guesses which made the game entertaining to play. Everybody deserves a thumbs up for sitting quietly and waiting patiently for a turn to speak during our game.”

Mr. Marcoscaife coughs and comments, “It never dawned on me that my students thought I could be so interesting, exciting and adventurous.” Next, he pulls out a DVD and reveals, “I also moonlight as a professional wheelchair bodybuilder.” DVD shows him lifting dumbbells, using a barbell and doing a posing routine set to “Muscles” by Diana Ross at a bodybuilding competition. It also shows Jean-Claude Van Damme spotting musclemen, Terry Crews pec bouncing and dancing, Arnold Schwarzenegger weightlifting at Venice Beach, famous wheelchair bodybuilders Nick Scott and Pasqualena Mitchell as well as Liam Hoekstra, the world’s strongest toddler, flexing his muscles.

After the DVD ends, Mr. Marcoscaife rolls up his sleeves and says, “I always wear long sleeves to cover the *shape* of my elbows. When I was growing in my mommy’s tummy, I elbowed her lots of times. I’m thankful to have elbows because they help my arms to move. However, no matter how big my muscles get, my dart-like elbows are still too *bony* and *pointy*.”

There's more to the story ...

Mr. Marcoscaife states, “Everyone has something on his or her body that he or she would like to change. For me, it’s my elbows, but, by the same token, I can laugh about them. My elbows remind me of two triangles with arrows: one pointing to the left and one pointing to the right. I’ve nicknamed them ‘the blinkers’ because to me, they look like they belong on the dashboard of a car.”

Turn the page for a bonus feature you don’t want to miss.

Story behind the story ...

Surprise! I'm the African-American *single* guy who inspired the story. Mr. Marcoscaife was created by extending my name, Marc Scaife. Growing up, Lady Canaday always said that my brother Larell and I had a natural form to be bodybuilders.

Long story short, I was a land walker before getting shot during the commission of an unsolved crime in 2007. Like the Caucasian teacher, I'm a wheelchair user and sported dreadlocks. However, the punch line of the story is purely a work of Lady Canaday's imagination. I have *normal-looking* elbows.

Printed in the United States
By Bookmasters